Clint and Grant
Play I-Spy

Level 1F

Written by Isabel Crawford
Illustrated by Stefania Maragna
Reading Consultant: Betty Franchi

About Phonics

Spoken English uses more than 40 speech sounds. Each sound is called a *phoneme*. Some phonemes relate to a single letter (d–o–g) and others to combinations of letters (sh–ar–p). When a phoneme is written down, it is called a *grapheme*. Teaching these sounds, matching them to their written form, and sounding out words for reading is the basis of phonics.

Early phonics instruction gives children the tools to sound out, blend, and say the words without having to rely on memory or guesswork. This instruction gives children the confidence and ability to read unfamiliar words, helping them progress toward independent reading.

About the Consultant

Betty Franchi is an American educator with a Bachelor's Degree in Elementary and Middle Education as well as a Master's Degree in Special Education. Betty holds a National Boards for Professional Teaching Standards certification. Throughout her 24 years as a teacher, she has studied and developed an expertise in Phonetic Awareness and has implemented phonetic strategies, teaching many young children to read, including students with special needs.

Reading tips

This book focuses on consonant, consonant, vowel, consonant, consonant words.

Tricky and/or new words in this book

Any words in bold may have unusual spellings or are new and have not yet been introduced.

> **Tricky and/or new words in this book**
>
> **see what sees eat bee with go they you the are of**

Extra ways to have fun with this book

After the readers have finished the story, ask them questions about what they have just read.

What did Clint see a bee do to the hens?
What was the duck wearing?

Make flashcards of the consonant, consonant, vowel, consonant, consonant words in this book. Ask the reader to say the words, sounding them out.
This will help reinforce letter/sound matches.

How many times can you see me in this book? More than once for sure!

A Pronunciation Guide

This grid highlights the sounds used in the story and offers a guide on how to say them.

s	a	t	p
as in sat	as in ant	as in tin	as in pig
i	n	c	e
as ink	as in net	as in cat	as in egg
h	r	m	d
as in hen	as in rat	as in mug	as in dog
g	o	u	l
as in get	as in ox	as in up	as in log
f	b	j	v
as in fan	as in bag	as in jug	as in van
w	z	y	k
as in wet	as in zip	as in yet	as in kit
qu	x	ff	ll
as in quick	as in box	as in off	as in ball
ss	zz	ck	
as in kiss	as in buzz	as in duck	

Be careful not to add an /uh/ sound to /s/, /t/, /p/, /c/, /h/, /r/, /m/, /d/, /g/, /l/, /f/ and /b/. For example, say /ff/ not /fuh/ and /sss/ not /suh/.

Let us **see what**
Clint and Grant spy.

Grant **sees** a tall, gruff man
in a small, red van.

Clint sees a **bee** put a spell
on a flock **of** hens. Buzz!

Grant sees a fat cat kiss
a cross rat in a fast van.

Clint sees an ox zip up
a cliff and pick a plant.

Grant sees a troll **eat**
grass as a snack.

Clint sees a duck drift past
in a skirt **with** frills.

Mom sees Grant and Clint **are** still up. "Quick, **go** to bed!"

Clint and Grant put **the** pencils back in the cup.

Off to bed **they** go.
What can **you** spy?

OVER **48** TITLES IN SIX LEVELS
Betty Franchi recommends...

Other titles to enjoy from Level 1

Bad Rat — I love reading phonics — 978 1 84898 747 0

The Best Gift — I love reading phonics — 978 1 84898 750 0

Bret and Grandma's Trip! — I love reading phonics — 978 1 84898 751 7

Some titles from Level 2

Wish Fish — I love reading phonics — 978 1 84898 755 5

Chuck and Duck — I love reading phonics — 978 1 84898 756 2

Pink Bunny — I love reading phonics — 978 1 84898 760 9

Let's go to the Swings — I love reading phonics — 978 1 84898 759 3

Some titles from Level 3

Bart's Go-Cart — I love reading phonics — 978 1 84898 768 5

Queen Ella's Feet — I love reading phonics — 978 1 84898 764 7

Puff Flies — I love reading phonics — 978 1 84898 765 4

The Pop Duet — I love reading phonics — 978 1 84898 767 8

An Hachette Company
First Published in the United States by TickTock, an imprint of Octopus Publishing Group.
www.octopusbooksusa.com

Copyright © Octopus Publishing Group Ltd 2013

Distributed in the US by
Hachette Book Group USA
237 Park Avenue, New York NY 10017, USA

Distributed in Canada by
Canadian Manda Group
165 Dufferin Street, Toronto, Ontario, Canada M6K 3H6

ISBN 978 1 84898 752 4

Printed and bound in China
10 9 8 7 6 5 4 3 2 1